Barb Holdridge

Porcupining
A Prickly Love Story

by LISA WHEELER

Illustrated by JANIE BYNUM

 LITTLE, BROWN AND COMPANY

New York ❧ Boston

For Shane, I couldn't pick a better son.
—Mom

With a special hug and a jar of love
for Janie B.
—L.W.

To my best friend Pam,
who loves me with all my quills!
—J.B.

Text copyright © 2002 by Lisa Wheeler
Illustrations copyright © 2002 by Janie Bynum

Little, Brown and Company

Time Warner Book Group
1271 Avenue of the Americas, New York, NY 10020
Visit our Web site at www.1b-kids.com

First Edition

Library of Congress Cataloging-in-Publication Data
Wheeler, Lisa.
    Porcupining : a prickly love story / by Lisa Wheeler ; illustrated by Janie Bynum. — 1st ed.
        p. cm.
    "Megan Tingley books."
    Summary: After a series of rejections, a lonely porcupine finds true love with a prickly hedgehog.
    ISBN 0-316-98912-6
    [1. Porcupines — Fiction. 2. Hedgehogs — Fiction.] I. Bynum, Janie, ill. II. Title.
PZ7.W5657 Po 2002
[E] — dc21   2001029654

10 9 8 7 6 5 4

TWP

Printed in Singapore

The illustrations for this book were done in digital watercolor and pastel.
The text was set in Schneidler and Aunt Mildred.

Cushion was a porcupine with a problem. He lived in a petting zoo. That was the problem. No one would pet a porcupine.

There were even signs outside his habitat that read:

DO NOT TOUCH and
KEEP OUT and worst of all
NO PETTING!

All the other animals got pats and pets and plenty of hugs. But not Cushion.

All the other animals had family and friends for company. But not Cushion.

All the other animals had someone to love. Poor Cushion had no one.

At night, Cushion got especially lonesome. He'd sit in the darkest corner of his house and feel sorry for himself. He even made up a sad, sad song.

I've been so lonesome all my life.
No one will get near.
I'm porcupining for a wife,
Someone to hold me dear.

After one especially long and lonesome night, Cushion decided he'd live alone no more.

"If a wife won't come looking for me, I'll go looking for a wife!"

So that night, when all the people went home and all the lights in the petting zoo went off, Cushion went poking around.

He tried finding a wife at the rabbit hutch. He sang his sad, sad song outside the door.

I've been so lonesome all my life,
I guess I can't be picky.
I'm porcupining for a wife,
And rabbits aren't too icky.

But for some reason, the rabbits got hopping mad and started poking fun at him.

"You're a walking burr-ball!" they teased. "Go away, *Pin*-Cushion!"

Cushion decided that rabbits were too jumpy and rude to make good companions. He wanted a wife who was easygoing, like him.

When he noticed the pink sow lazing in the pigsty,
he decided to try again.
He sang his sad, sad song.

I've been so lonesome all my life,
And though you're pink and fat,
I'm porcupining for a wife,
So I won't mention that.

But for some reason, the sow just grunted and turned her back on him. Cushion got the point. "Must be stuck-up," he decided. "I'll find a wife who has a sharper sense of humor."

So he tried the beavers' lodge. They always seemed to be in a good mood.

When he spied a beaver swimming in the water, Cushion sang his sad, sad song.

I've been so lonesome all my life,
And though your teeth are bucky,
I'm porcupining for a wife,
So you're a gal who's lucky.

But for some reason, the beaver didn't appreciate Cushion's song. She started needling him.

"No girl in her right mind would marry you, you scrub brush!" And with a slap of her tail on the water — *SPLASH* — she swam away.

Cushion, soaking wet and getting discouraged, tried to console himself.

"I know I'll find the perfect wife if I just stick with it."

Suddenly, he heard a voice nearby. "Psssst! Hey, you!"
Cushion turned his head toward the voice. "Me?"
"Yes, you," whispered the voice. "I heard you singing tonight.
You have a lovely voice."
Cushion tried to see who was speaking. He leaned closer to
the sound.

"Stop right there!" said the voice. "Can't you read the signs?"
Cushion looked up and read:

DO NOT TOUCH and
KEEP OUT and worst of all
NO PETTING!

He felt a prickle run down his spine.

"Who are you?" asked Cushion.

"My name is Barbara," said the sweet, clear voice. "But you can
call me Barb."

"Barb is a beautiful name," said Cushion. "Are you dangerous?"

"I don't think so," said Barb. "Are you?"

"I'm a porcupine," said Cushion. "I've got quills."

"I've got quills, too!" Barb announced as she stepped into
the light. "I'm a hedgehog."

Standing there before him was a quaint, quilled creature.

"You don't look like a hedge or a hog!" said Cushion.
"You're beautiful!"

"And you don't look like pork or a pine!" said Barb. "You're
outstanding!"

Cushion's heart was overflowing. He felt this was the perfect moment to sing Barb his sad, sad song — which suddenly didn't seem sad at all!

I've been so lonesome all my life.
Now I've met Barb, so fair.
I'm porcupining for a wife —
We'd make a perfect pair.

And of course, they did!

(Or what would be the point of this whole story?)